It Was Always You

A 1Night Stand Story

By
Tianna Xander

Copyright © 2016 by Tianna Xander
ISBN: 978-1-68361-025-0
Cover art by Fiona Jayde

Published by Decadent Publishing Company LLC
Look for us online at:
www.decadentpublishing.com

Praise for *It Was Always You*

Took me by surprise and had me flipping the pages from beginning to end ~ Amazon Reviewer

A dream come true, something we all want. Our heroine gets hers in this story. There is mystery, passion, Heartbreak and then resolution ~ Amazon Reviewer

Brilliantly entertaining read! 5 Stars all the way!! ~ Amazon Reviewer

Tianna Xander weaves a romantic tale that had her readers wondering what will happen of these two star struck lovers ~ Amazon Reviewer

Fantasy and happily-ever-after come true in this romantic tale with a paranormal twist. A delightful read ~ Amazon Reviewer

Great dynamic characters, good story, and steamy scenes had me reading through the night ~ Amazon Reviewer

~A Note from the Author~

What woman hasn't dreamed their movie-star crush will suddenly appear in their life and sweep them off their feet? Does anyone believe that can happen? As an erotic romance author, I've probably imagined that scenario more than most—if only from an author's point of view.

After coming to terms with the fact that I too have a crush on a movie star, I imagined *It Was Always You*, as the embodiment of those daydreams, night dreams, and possibly wet dreams for each and every one of us. Who doesn't want their favorite movie stars to suddenly realize they can't live without us no matter who we are or what we look like on the outside?

I hope you enjoy reading the story as much as I enjoyed writing it.

Tianna

www.tiannaxander.com

Dedication

To dreamers everywhere

Chapter One

The loud jangle of the phone ripped Candy from one of the best dreams she'd ever had. She'd dreamt of *him* again, her favorite actor and fantasy lover rolled into one. After having them for so long, she couldn't remember when they had started. She only knew they got hotter and hotter.

Her heart raced every time she touched Jared Harwell in her little visions. Her breathing hitched, and her clit throbbed, aching with the need to come. He'd brought her so close to climax this time and then the damned phone had to ring. Tempted to throw the offending object out the second-story window, she rolled over and grabbed the receiver.

"Hello." Candy didn't keep her irritation from her voice. She couldn't. Every damned time, someone, or something, dragged her from the fantasy which could very well make her life complete.

"At least you're not dead," her best friend and neighbor, Samantha James said.

"What the heck are you talking about?" Pushing to a sitting position, Candy leaned against the headboard, closed her eyes, and wished she'd unplugged the phone the night before.

"You've had a man pounding on your front door for the last ten minutes. Don't you hear him?"

She canted her head and listened. "I don't hear anything."

"The poor guy gave up. He sat down in your rocker with a suitcase in his lap." Samantha paused. "Do you have a tall, dark, and handsome brother I don't know about?"

"Uh, *no*." Sam knew better than that. "The fact that I just received a sizeable inheritance from my grandmother's estate should have told you something."

"Yeah, well, a girl can hope." Sam sighed. "He sure is something to look at. And why is he carrying a suitcase?"

"I have no idea." Candy slid from her bed, donned an old, comfortable bathrobe then sat at her desk.

She moved the mouse, and the computer screen lit

up, showing her she had a new email from the 1Night Stand agency.

Her stomach did a flip. She'd taken some of her inheritance money and paid to have the fantasy of a lifetime. She'd described Jared Harwell on her application and thought it possible that having a fling with someone who resembled him would get him out of her system. Pining after some movie star for the rest of her life couldn't be healthy.

"What are you doing, sitting at your desk?" Sam shouted. "Go answer your door."

"Why? Whoever the guy is, he's at the wrong house. He'll figure that out soon enough. And stop spying on me with that stinking telescope of yours."

Candy clicked on the subject line and opened her mail. It contained instructions, telling her to meet her *date* at a hotel in Ottawa during some kind of author/reader event called Romancing the Capital.

April seventeenth! That's tomorrow. I can't possibly be in Ottawa tomorrow. Hell, it barely gave her time to make travel arrangements.

"I don't think he plans to go anywhere any time soon. He just leaned back in the chair and crossed his legs. I think he's gonna wait you out."

Candy, always multitasking, read further.

Apparently, she should expect a courier, who would hand deliver a plane ticket and the information about her date. The letter also informed her she had one shot at this. Her date could not and would not reschedule. One chance only.

Sighing, she shifted the phone to her other ear. "I have to go, Sam. I'll call you back as soon as I can." Setting the phone down, she pushed away from the desk, pulled her robe tighter, and headed for the stairs. She couldn't screw this up. A friend at work had told her about Madame Eve, the mysterious Frenchwoman and owner of 1Night Stand, who seemed to *know* who to pair with whom.

Like magic, Madame Eve nearly always managed to put two people together who got along famously. The rumors in Candy's circle of friends were the woman had some sort of psychic ability, or she used magic—if one believed in such a thing.

Why shouldn't she believe? After having visualized her ideal lover for the last several months, she'd begun to wonder if the two of them had some sort of real psychic connection. She'd fantasized Jared had somehow been aware of what he did in his sleep, much as she had been. What if he'd also mastered the art of lucid dreaming not long after her nightly visits

with him began? Every night she lived her fantasies—
if only in her sleep.

"They found someone who matches my
description." She danced toward the stairs, giddy.

Seriously, what were the odds a man who
resembled the one she wanted in her life would need
the services of the 1Night Stand agency? She'd lay
odds Jared Harwell never wanted for female
companionship for even one day in his charmed,
movie-star life. She had a difficult time imagining
anyone matching *his* description would have a hard
time finding dates.

"But, tomorrow?" She bit her lip. It gave her
almost *no* time to prepare. She hoped Madame Eve
really *had* worked everything out.

*You have had the last six months to prepare,
Candy. Suck it up, otherwise all of this will have
been for nothing.* Not to mention the fact she would
lose her only chance at her fantasy.

Pausing at the front door, she brushed her hair
back, smoothed down the front of the oversized robe,
and reached for the knob.

A tall, forty-something Adonis with dark hair and
sky-blue eyes stood on her front porch, just out of the
early-morning spring sunlight. Sam had been right.

He *was* gorgeous, even if he didn't look like her dream lover. Had Candy not already been in love with Jared Harwell, the guy before her could very well be someone she'd go for. *In a heartbeat.*

The low-slung sports car parked at the curb didn't mark him as a commercial courier. If she had to guess, she'd peg him as a successful businessman. Maybe the owner of 1Night Stand had her fingers in a little bit of everything and called in favors as she needed them.

What do I know?

"Yes?" She tried to catch her breath as he handed her an envelope and set a medium-sized suitcase at her feet.

"Candy Williamson?" At her nod, he continued, "My name is Jamie. Your 1Night Stand date sent me to give this to you. It contains instructions, along with your plane ticket. I've been told you're to open and read the first page in my presence. I'm to get affirmation that you understand the rules of the game before I leave."

"Game? I thought this was—"

"Your fantasy come true?" He smiled. "It is, but it's also a fantasy for your date. Apparently, things work both ways. These are the terms set forth by the

6

gentleman in question."

With trembling fingers, she ripped open the envelope, and, following the instructions on the first line, read the rest of it aloud. "The courier should have arrived with a bag for you. Do not, under any circumstances, open the case before you reach Ottawa. If you prefer, the courier will remove it and have it sent to await you at the hotel. I understand if you do not wish to carry the bag with you since you do not know what it contains."

She glanced down at the bag and nodded. "Yeah. No offense, but I could be smuggling drugs across the border in that thing. I might have thought about it if I could open it, but since I can't…. No, thanks."

She grinned. "But mostly, I want you to take it because I *would* open it before tomorrow night. My curiosity over what's inside it would get the best of me." Chuckling, she added, "I have absolutely *no* willpower. I know this about myself."

"Then I'll be happy to take it with me." Her early-morning visitor winked. "I think he expected you to turn the case down. Most people won't carry a bag that's not theirs onto a plane, and those who do are just asking for trouble. I suspect your date just wanted you to wonder what he's got hidden inside it."

He tilted his head and stared at her for a moment. "Judging by your expression, the mission has been accomplished." Hands behind his back, he nodded toward the letter. "Is there more?"

"You know there is." She glanced at the paper then back at him. "Why do I think you know exactly what this says?"

"Because you're an astute woman?" He raised a brow.

"More like because I'm a suspicious one," she laughed. A noise behind him caught her attention. She leaned to her right to look around the handsome man and waved at her nosy neighbor. "Oh hello, Mrs. Wendt." Lowering her voice, Candy whispered, "Tomorrow, the entire neighborhood will know you were here. I hope you're single because the rumors *that* lady can spread would make any girl jealous, even of me. I wouldn't be surprised if she has already taken photos of you and your car to post on the Internet."

"There's nothing wrong with you, miss. And photos of me are already on the 'net." He gestured to the page in her hand with a half-smile. "You might want to continue. I'm to report back to Mr. Right that you've read it."

"Is that his name—*Mr. Right?*" How funny that would be, if it were so.

"No." He shook his head with a laugh. "That is most certainly *not* his name. He wishes to remain anonymous until your night together. He also wants to be certain that you are well aware of his wishes." The courier rested a hand on her shoulder. "I know you have no reason to trust me, but I will tell you he is trustworthy, and Madame Eve would never set you up with someone who would harm you. The safety of her clients is always on her mind. She has handpicked every match since starting 1Night Stand and yours is no different."

Candy's stomach lurched at his little speech. Glancing back at the paper in her hand, she began reading aloud, once more. "After your plane arrives, take the waiting car to the hotel then go to your room and relax. At precisely midnight, open the bag, dress in the clothing and wear the blindfold provided, and wait for me on the bed. Under no circumstances are you to remove the mask unless you fear for your safety or I say you may do so. Otherwise, removing it voids our agreement."

She thought about the instructions. "Wait a minute. The whole reason I wanted someone with his

9

description is because I wanted to *look* at him, damn it." Fisting her hands on her hips, she frowned, not giving a damn if she wrinkled the precious letter from *Mr. Right*. Why did he think *he* had the right to call all of the shots? Who had Madame Eve found to play the part of Jared Harwell in her little fantasy? Whoever Candy had gotten, he certainly seemed full of himself.

"Those are his instructions." The courier shrugged. "Maybe he just wants you to concentrate on who *he* is for a little while, instead of you imagining he's the fellow you really want. I do know he does intend to let you see him before your time is over. I just can't tell you when."

"You work for him, don't you?" She narrowed her eyes.

"Guilty." He raised his hand and smiled again. "The only thing I am allowed to tell you is, if you follow his instructions, you won't be sorry." Bending, he picked up the case and turned to go. Halfway down her porch steps, he glanced back. "There is one more thing he didn't tell me I *couldn't* say."

Glowering, she asked, "What would that be?" The instructions had given her plenty to think about. She'd paid what she considered a lot of money for the date. Shouldn't *she* be demanding a few things of her own?

"Your date looks forward to your time together. More than you know." Striding to his car, her visitor unceremoniously dumped the case in the back and slid into the driver's seat. He put the car in gear, waved through the moon roof, and hit the gas, tires protesting the fast take-off with a loud screech.

She stared after him, her bottom lip between her teeth. Looking down at the letter, she read it again and frowned then headed back inside. What should she do about *Mr. Right* and his strange demands? Should she trust Madame Eve and her matchmaking skills, or she call the whole thing off?

Chapter Two

"Did you deliver the letter as instructed?" Jared leaned back in his chair, crossed his arms, and stared up at his personal assistant, who leaned against the doorjamb. Jared had planned the date to the last detail and wanted everything perfect.

"You know I did." James pushed away from the door, shoved his keys in his pocket, and sat across from his best friend. "It's a good thing she agreed to it. Meeting her in Ottawa fits into your busy schedule perfectly."

"Yes. Being up there for a few days at that romance thing gives both of us some downtime, too. It works out well. I can spend a time in the country unwinding before and after."

"You'll probably need it after a day in a room full of oversexed women."

Jared stared at his best friend and raised a brow. "I seem to recall you used to like situations like that."

"That was before you got famous, and speaking of that, I don't know why you don't tell your date who you are right off the bat." Jamie shrugged. "Any lass would be lucky to have you for the night, if you ask me."

Jared shook his head and sighed. He wished he'd known it would be more bother than it was worth before he'd set himself on this path. James never understood the problems he faced with his celebrity status. Not that it mattered a hell of a lot. He only had another five years at most before he had to quit. Otherwise, someone would notice he never aged.

Sometimes he wondered what it would be like to be able to return to a life of anonymity. A life where he could be certain a person stayed in his life because they cared about him, not because of what he could do for them.

"And I have no doubt in my mind she would think the same. I want some time to get to know her before she finds out who I am. I want her to see the man, not the movie star. Is that too much to ask?" It didn't really matter. He only had the one night with the woman.

Why did others find it so difficult to understand he wanted his date to like him for himself, not what he could do or buy for them? He was never certain of the real reasons a girl dated him. Did she really like him, or did she just find his bank account attractive?

In a perfect world, he would meet and marry someone who had never heard of Jared Harwell. However, *that* would be next to impossible. His face was on too many magazines and on too many TVs to remain anonymous for any length of time.

He had employed the 1Night Stand agency to set up the little fantasy for him to keep his anonymity. He needed to let off some steam with a female *he* found hot before he went on the hunt for the perfect Hollywood wife. He never had understood the media's habit of attacking a woman because of her size. So what if he found heavier women attractive? It should be his business and no one else's. Still, Jared knew he couldn't subject a woman, especially a woman who he might come to care about, to such heartless bastards.

"I don't suppose so. But if you want my opinion, she isn't the kind of chick to go for you just because you're famous. She asked for someone fitting your description. That should count for something."

"You just don't get it, do you? *I'm* probably her fantasy." Jared snorted and ran his fingers through his hair. "God, that sounded conceited, didn't it?"

He hated celebrities who let their fame go to their heads. Though, he wasn't sure he hadn't become one of them over the last few years.

Pushing away from his desk, he stood. "I don't think it's too much to ask that I make sure the person I intend to spend time with, even for one night, wants me for me. Do you?"

"I don't suppose it is." James frowned. "Are you going to let her hear your accent or are you going to sound like an American? You know she specifically requested someone with either an English or Scottish accent."

"I haven't decided yet." He rubbed the back of his neck and stared out his penthouse window. "I know she wanted an accent. I've been thinking I can sound American, and when she complains that I have a Midwestern accent, I can switch to one of the others and make it seem as though I'm an American who just happens to do accents very well."

"Your voice coaches were good. They say you could pass for an American any day."

"They've done the same for you, Jamie Campbell."

Jared grinned. It shouldn't be difficult. They'd been passing for humans for years.

"She didn't suspect a thing, either." Jamie chuckled. "I spoke with the perfect American accent, and she didn't bat an eye."

"Was she pretty?" Jared planned to respect the rules Madame Eve had set in her email to him and not contact the woman further, but he really wanted to know if his date at least resembled the girl he had in mind. He supposed she must. It had been one of his few requirements, after all.

"*You* would think so." James shrugged. It didn't escape Jared's notice that, as usual, Jamie had no personal opinion about a female he found attractive. They both acted as though they had some unwritten code that neither of them would consider a girl the other found appealing. Still, Jamie's taste in women ran along the same lines as Jared's own. "She's in her mid-to-late forties, golden hair, and eyes the color of new blue jeans."

"I wish you had gotten a photo."

"I did, but it's not a good one. I snapped it with my phone as I waved good-bye from the car. I didn't want to make it obvious."

"Well, show it to me, ye ass." Jared couldn't wait

to get a glimpse of her. Even if the picture didn't do her justice, he might be able to tell if it was her haunting his nights for the last seven months. "How can ye have a photo of the lass and not tell me as soon as ye walk through the door?"

"Calm down, *Mr. Right*. Your accent is showing." James laughed outright. "I wanted you to stew about it for a bit. I'm glad I did. You should have seen your reaction."

Jamie dug his phone from his pocket, pulled the image up, and handed it over.

"It's difficult to tell." He studied the screen. "The hair color is right, but her body shape seems all wrong." He frowned. "And there's no way to know if the hair is dyed or natural."

His dream lover was natural all the way down to the golden curls between her legs. Was this woman the same?

"The color is her own, believe me. She has crystal-blonde eyebrows." James stared at the picture for a moment and frowned. "I don't know how you can make out *any* body shape with that huge bathrobe she's got on."

Jared frowned at the image and grunted. "Is that what she's wearing?"

"Yes. That's definitely what it is. It hung off her like a gunnysack. I'd daresay it belonged to her last lover." He grinned. "I'm not sure, but I think I woke her up. Her mussed hair gave her away, and her eyes had that just woken-up look. Hell, she might have had a lover waiting in her bed, for all I know."

"I don't care to hear about her lovers." It was bad enough he'd only have a short time with her before he went off and found himself some young, pretty thing, one he had nothing in common with, to marry.

"Uh...Jared?" James ran a finger under his collar. "As much as I'd like to see you happy, aren't you afraid what the media will say about you seeing someone like this lass?"

Jared narrowed his eyes. "What do you mean? I don't plan to date her. One night—one weekend, if I'm lucky, and I will be back to dating the kind of waif the media approves of." He curled his lip. "I'm rich and I'm famous. You would think I could marry whoever the fuck I want to."

Instead, if he wasn't careful, he'd end up wedded to a mere slip of a girl who would fit the media's, and everyone else's, idea of the perfect match for him. What good came of being rich and famous if a person let the world dictate what they could and couldn't do with their lives? What a crock of shit his life had become if he let that happen.

All he ever wanted was to find his mate and be happy. Instead, he'd set on this path of self-destruction as a celebrity. Maybe, he shouldn't give a shit about his career and what marrying out of the Hollywood celebrity norm could do to it. Perhaps he should tell everyone to kiss his ass and marry whoever the hell he wanted. It wasn't as though it would matter unless he got lucky and found his mate.

Like that will ever happen.

"I couldn't care less who you fuck, as long as she makes you happy. You know that, right?" Jamie held his hands up. "I don't mean to insult the lass. You know my tastes in the opposite sex are the same as yours, but if the media finds out you're seeing someone like her, even for one night, they'll have a field day tearing her down. All I'm saying is, I'm not sure it's fair to her."

"I'll do whatever I can to keep her out of the limelight. I don't want to scar her with other's insults. I merely want to know what it's like to spend time with the kind of girl *I* find attractive." It had been years since he'd been able to do that with anyone who'd attracted him physically as well as stimulated him mentally.

Once married, he intended to be faithful to his partner. He just wanted one night to pretend he could have a life with the kind of female he found attractive. Unfortunately, James was right—the public would tear both of them apart if it got the slightest scent of any romance between him and a woman it deemed less than perfect for him. It didn't matter what he thought. It never had.

Chapter Three

C andy climbed out of the limo and followed the driver as he carried her luggage into the hotel. She headed for the front desk and waited in line behind a group of women who were, no doubt, part of the romance convention. She glanced around the sumptuous lobby. It fell right in line with the decadent flight Madame Eve had arranged. She'd gone all out, purchasing first-class plane tickets for Candy, and now, luxury accommodations. She could only imagine what room the matchmaker had rented her for the night.

If this place has a presidential suite, it's probably where I'll be spending the night. What a waste, though. Because, if everything went the way she wanted, Candy wouldn't notice any more of her room than the bed.

"Excuse me, miss?" A hand landed on her arm,

gently turning her toward the masculine voice. "Are you Candy Williamson?" Tall and dark, the man wore a nice suit with a nametag identifying him as *Michael S, Assistant Manager*. Boy-next-door looks lit up with his smile, his brown eyes reminding her of melted dark chocolate.

"Yes. Yes I am. What can I do for you?" She frowned when he snapped his fingers at a nearby young man and pointed to her luggage. Certainly, they didn't have bellhops. Weren't those a thing of the past? She didn't remember the last time anyone other than herself had carried her bags.

"We have special instructions to escort you to your room." Michael smiled down at her. "Your friend wanted a specific suite, and it had already been reserved for the night."

All business, he added, "We have managed to resituate the other guest and grant the request. It has a hot tub en suite, a sitting area, and two bedrooms."

They stepped from the elevator and headed toward the room. The bellhop unlocked the door and went in ahead of her.

"Where would you like your bags?"

Ignoring him, Candy couldn't help but stare through the doorway of the first bedroom at the suitcase her messenger had brought her the morning before, in the middle of the large bed. The only thing the letter had told her the case contained was a blindfold. Whatever other secrets it held would remain a mystery until midnight. She could ignore the case for a few hours—she'd make certain of it.

"Just leave them by the door," she said. "I'll take care of them myself, thank you." She fumbled in her purse, hoping to find tip money to give to the bellhop. "Good grief. Don't tell me I don't have any cash." she muttered.

"Don't worry about a gratuity, Ms. Williamson. They've been taken care of for the weekend. Just relax and enjoy yourself." Michael handed her the keycard he had used to open the door, and, with a nod to the other man to follow him, left.

"Thank you." Candy stared at the closed door for several moments before grabbing her bags and lugging them into the room where the mysterious suitcase sat in the middle of the bed, looking for all the world like a bomb in a subway. Her imagination ran wild with ideas of what could be in the damned thing.

She fisted her hands at her sides, her fingers itching to open it and find out what secrets it held.

Instead, she managed a little willpower and moved the bags she'd brought with her to the luggage rack. Striding to the dresser, she found an envelope, addressed to her, sitting next to the TV.

Dearest Candy,

I look forward to meeting you later this evening. I trust you will follow my instructions to the letter. Please understand, I have no wish to frighten or harm you, I merely want you to experience me as myself before you fantasize I am whoever you wish me to be. Be certain, I will do the same for you.

Take your time and relax before our evening together. Feel free to help yourself to the mini-bar. All expenses will be covered.

Until tonight,

Mr. Right

"Heh. A poet and didn't know it." She chuckled at his two-sentence rhyme. Tossing the letter back onto the dresser, she turned toward the bed and her suitcases. "Well, if I had any doubt *Mr. Right* meant for this room to be mine, I guess that's out." She opened the closest drawer and gaped at the men's clothing inside. Another note sat atop the neatly folded items.

Candy,

Please use the drawers on the other side. Though I plan to stay a few more days, I had hoped to share this room with you tonight. I don't want to waste a moment of it apart.

R

I guess I'll have no privacy this weekend.

She frowned. If he *did* stay here with her, where the hell did he expect her to stay after tonight? A couch in the lobby?

Sighing, she opened the drawer farthest from her. Should she bother unpacking her bag? She'd only have to move them in the morning since she'd have just the one night with him, after all. But, unpacking seemed like instructions, and she had agreed to follow his instructions for the night. With another little sigh, she neatly arranged her clothes in the drawers he'd left to her.

Her other bag held all the nice things she needed to hang. Opening the closet door, she was surprised to find a large walk-in. About a quarter of the space held men's clothing. He'd brought much more than one guy could wear in a weekend. Did he plan to stay longer than just a few days?

Did he have more than one of these fantasies set up? She panicked a little at the thought. Had he seen her and already written their night off as a bad move?

Stop second-guessing a man you haven't met yet. Being her own worst critic tended to be her greatest flaw. Deep down, she was certain no one had found her difficult to look at, but thoughts of her size kept rearing their ugly heads and ruining everything for her.

Glancing at the clock, she gasped. She'd taken much longer than anticipated unpacking the other case. In a hurry, she haphazardly hung her things on the other side of the closet then dragged in her overnight bag to get it out of the way.

I need a shower.

Chapter Four

Jared unlocked the door and entered the suite, not bothering to hit the light switch. He'd spent the last several hours imagining what his date looked like and didn't know if he wanted to find out, the reason he hadn't turned on the light. Though he'd meant what he'd said in his letter about getting to know her, he still wanted the woman he'd described to Madame Eve on his application. But what if she couldn't measure up to his fantasy?

What if I don't measure up to hers?

One of his main fears was disappointing her. He'd never understood why females were so attracted to him, and he'd never taken it for granted a girl would like him. Perhaps it had something to do with his werewolf pheromones.

So, he had one shot at this. As he'd said on his

application to 1Night Stand, he had no intention of doing this sort of thing ever again. It was now, or never. He'd planned the evening as his last chance to live the life he'd once thought to have, before resigning himself to the life people expected him to live. Just as he didn't want his date going into this with any preconceived notions, he refused to fall into the same trap.

The darkness would give them a fair chance. At least that's what he hoped.

Entering the bedroom, he frowned. *It's too quiet.* Had she left?

"Candy?" he whispered. If she expected him, the movie star, she would recognize his voice. He had to remember to speak with a Midwestern accent at a low level and not have his brogue give him away. Not yet, anyway. He said her name softly again.

No answer.

"Candy, are you there?" he asked a bit louder. Had his accent bled through? It didn't matter. His instructions had probably scared her, and she'd left. *Shit!*

"Huh, wha...?" The sleep-filled voice came from the bed. "Who's there?"

"It's just me, darlin'. Your date for the evening."

"Why are you whispering?" The sheets rustled. She'd turned off the lights as he'd instructed in his letter. With the curtains drawn, the glow from the city below couldn't penetrate the darkness. *That* hadn't been part of his conditions. Had she'd closed them to even the playing field so he couldn't see her either?

Standing in the doorway, he breathed in her perfume. The scent of peaches wafted up from the bed and gave him a hard-on from hell. The sweet scent filled his lungs. He closed his eyes and inhaled deeply, the lingering scent bringing up sweet memories of *his* Candy. Still, it didn't matter. The only thing he gave a damn about—they get along with each other and have the fantasy they wanted.

"Have you changed your mind?" He hoped not, and pictured the lingerie he'd packed in the case for her. Had she put it on, or was she wearing something of her own?

"No, I haven't changed my mind. I'm wearing the flimsy nightgown you sent for me, aren't I?" she asked, dryly.

How could he know what she wore? He could barely see the shape of his bloody hand in front of his face.

"Uh, yes. Yes, if you say so, I guess you are," he replied, relieved she wore what he'd given her, though he couldn't see her. He could only imagine her as his fantasy lover in the silky gown. Perhaps the darkness would serve him better. That way, she could be anything, anyone he wanted. He'd be able to touch her, and tonight, nothing else mattered.

"It fits as though someone made it for me. Did someone tell you my size?"

Uncertainty filled her voice. Most likely, she wondered if she knew him.

"I don't know you outside of this room, if that's what you're asking." He'd had no idea whether the gown would fit or not, but known it would have fit his dream lover like a glove since he knew every inch of *her* body better than he knew his own. "I bought the gown for a woman I think is perfect for me."

He moved closer to the bed, removed his jacket, and yanked his shirt over his head, tossing them both toward the wall. Hitting something with a whack, they dropped to the floor, followed by his belt buckle striking the carpet with a muffled thud.

"I take it that was some article of clothing hitting the TV set," she said. "Can you hurry this along? I'm really nervous, and I'm having a difficult time not reaching for the mask. To tell you the truth, I'm kind of scared, and the blindfold doesn't help."

"Then take it off. Just don't turn on the light." Jared kept his voice light. Unbuttoning his pants, he kicked them off, along with his trainers. Thank God for shoes that slipped off without a hitch.

"Thank you." The sheets rustled, and he imagined her ripping the blindfold from her face. "It's beginning to make me itch."

Jared wanted to make her itch in another way. He also prayed that the fact she wore the gown meant she intended to go through with the sexual side of the date. It was one of the things he'd said he wanted. He wouldn't attempt to force the issue if she said no, though. Anything that happened between them would be up to her.

He moved closer, following her glorious scent. "I've fantasized about you all night. I wanted to get up here earlier, but I had a previous engagement I couldn't get out of.

"I'm going to touch you now." He bent toward her.

"I know." Her breath hitched. "I can see you."

"You can?" He paused. She couldn't possibly see him clearly if the darkness made it impossible for him to get a glimpse of her. His kind had exceptional eyesight. Reaching out, he gently stroked her hair. *It's just as soft as I'd hoped.*

"Well...I can see your silhouette. I can't really see much other than you're big."

"I thought you wanted someone rather large." He swallowed, almost afraid to continue, but he had to know where things stood. Not that he could do much about it now. Over six feet tall, he *wasn't* small. That was certain. And he worked out regularly, since staying in shape helped him land the roles that had made him famous. "You know, it occurred to me, I just waltzed in here and took my clothes off as though we'd get right down to business without getting to know each other at least somewhat. Are you comfortable with this or should we wait?"

"Yes." She fidgeted a bit. "Unless you're asking because you've changed your mind."

"Not on your life, lady." He stroked the hair from her forehead.

"Good. Can I touch your face?"

"Of course." He smiled slightly. She'd wanted him clean shaven, but he'd left a bit of stubble. Shaving would have uncovered the scar on his chin. The peculiar, raised, crescent-shaped scar would have given him away, if she watched his movies.

32

Her hands cupped his cheeks. "I'm glad you didn't shave, even though I asked for that. This is better. Sexier."

"We can't always get what we want," he said, quietly. If they could, he would be settling down with someone like her instead of facing an empty life with someone he didn't want.

She ran her fingers over his forehead, eyes, and nose.

He nipped the tips of them when they reached his mouth. "It's my turn now. Can I touch you?" Not waiting for a reply, he took her hands in his, leaned down, and pressed his face into the crook of her neck. "Anywhere?"

"Yes." She spoke as softly as he did. "I don't know why we're whispering, and I don't care. It's sexy. Knowing that this...thing is only for one night is sexy, too." She breathed a little sigh. "It makes me feel kind of easy, but I don't care." Arching, she pressed her breasts into his face.

Jared groaned. "You smell amazing." What was it about her? It couldn't just be her perfume. The familiar scent of the peach body butter *his* fantasy woman used mixed in with the amazing aroma of Candy Williamson made him react in such a strange way. What made him want her so badly? He wanted her more than he'd ever thought possible.

He cupped her full breasts. True to her word, she wore the gown he'd purchased for the night he would spend with his dream lover. It no longer mattered who this woman happened to be in real life. She smelled right, the stroke of his fingers against her smooth flesh felt right. She sounded right. Maybe he should have called himself Mr. Desperate and named *her* Miss Right.

Because Jared *was* desperate. He'd needed and lived for this date since he'd received the email from Madame Eve informing him she had found the perfect applicant for him. His mystery woman had asked for a guy fitting his description. In his excitement, he'd imagined she could very well be the one from his lonely nights. Not that it would matter. They had no future. He'd known it going in.

He swallowed thickly as he caressed Candy's soft skin. After this night, his fantasies were all he would have left.

Jared had no idea why this woman gave him the strange sense of belonging he'd searched for over the last several years. *Stop imagining things you shouldn't, Jared. This has no future.*

Leaning down, he gently touched his lips to hers. Her mouth opened beneath his, her tongue darting out to taste him. Desire and a sense of finally belonging exploded over him. His breathing grew heavy as her touch left his face, her arms wrapping around his neck to draw him closer.

He lost himself in the kiss, in her wonderful, addicting scent. This woman, dream lover or not, had already rocked his world. He would have to make the most of the time they had together.

Chapter Five

Candy stared up into the darkness. The man's face stayed nothing more than a dark shape. She took a deep breath, loving his citrusy scent. Finding a bottle of aftershave on the counter in the bathroom when she showered earlier, she'd discovered she liked it.

"You don't have an accent." She had no idea if she should be disappointed or not. She had wanted her fantasy, but the reality could turn out so much better.

"Would you like me to have one?" he asked, using the staid English speech used in Shakespearean plays. "I could always talk like this, if you prefer."

"No. You sound fine." She *liked* the way he sounded—even without the brogue she'd thought she'd wanted at first. "I think it's better that we aren't pretending. I like you just the way you are."

Maybe she'd matured a little and her subconscious

mind had accepted this man because, deep down, she could never have the one of her dreams. Jared Harwell would always be too famous to give someone like her the time of day. Hell, she would probably be lucky to get the actor's attention long enough to get an autograph.

Mystery Man kissed her again, deeper than before. His tongue tangled with hers for a moment before he sucked it into his mouth, tugging gently until she melted against him.

Candy roamed her hands over his hard-muscled body as their tongues dueled and their lips frantically clashed together. He pressed his hips against hers, the thick ridge of his cock straining against her abdomen.

Slowly, she slid her fingers over his warm skin, the tips gliding over the valleys between his well-formed muscles. *Mr. Right* had the body of a male stripper, and that only turned her on more. Her body already cried for the release she knew he'd give her.

Large, callused palms explored her body—those of a laborer, maybe a carpenter. He touched her almost reverently, his fingers sliding over the swell of her breasts, down to the ample curves of her waist and still farther down to her hips. Gliding his palms beneath her ass, he grasped her cheeks and squeezed.

"I love the way you feel in my arms—so soft and inviting." he said quietly.

"I could say the same about you, Mystery Man. You're all hard and hot, but you feel so good," she said. She liked the fact he hadn't raised his voice above a whisper. It seemed sexy, decadent, almost as though they hid from something, or lent an air of danger to their time together. "I love the way your muscles ripple when I touch them."

Reaching behind him, she gripped his hard ass, scoring the cheeks and his upper thighs with her nails. He groaned, his hips thrusting against her.

"How did you know I would like that?" He followed the question with another deep groan.

"I didn't. I just knew *I* would." Candy grinned into the darkness. She wrapped one leg around him, pushing her mound tighter against him, urging him on.

Part of her wished she had the courage to tell him to forgo the condoms, if he dared, but she had more brains than to consider it for more than a minute.

"The condoms are in the drawer."

"I know." He chuckled. "I checked when I came in."

So that's what he'd been doing. She'd sensed his presence next to her, had even thought she'd heard the drawer of the nightstand open and close.

Lowering his head, he drew her left nipple into his mouth, his silky hair brushing her skin. He sucked deeply and nipped as his tongue flicked over the sensitive tip. His scratchy, short beard only added to the fire growing inside her as he tugged the sensitized nub, causing her to shiver and moan.

"Do you like that?"

He needn't have asked her the question. She arched her reply, her body striving to follow the stroke of his rough cheek as he pulled away from her.

"Well?"

"You know I did," she answered, a bit disgruntled. This was *her* fantasy, too, after all. "Are you going to tease me all night, or are we going to get busy?"

God, did that just sound cheap, or what?

He moved back to her breast, rubbing his rough cheek across it, the friction nearly driving her mad. "Aren't you happy with the way things are moving along?" He breathed the words, his tongue darting out to flick over her nipples once again. Alternating between them, he sucked one while gently twisting the other between his fingers. He kept her on the verge of climax for what could have been an eternity, but surely no more than a few minutes.

Her head thrashed on the pillow. "Of course I'm happy. You *are* my fantasy, after all." She stroked his muscular shoulders, over his back, all too aware she didn't care who made her body react the way it did. She didn't care what he looked like—*who* he looked like anymore. At the moment, the only thing she gave a damn about was getting him to give her an orgasm at least once before he drove her mad.

But she needed him to experience the same urgency she did. Reaching between them, she wrapped her fingers around his thick length, grazing her fingers over his shaft, careful not to scrape with her nails. She cupped his sac, squeezing his balls gently as he mindlessly thrust his hips against her.

"Don't make me lose control, darlin'." He groaned. "I'm not as young as I used to be. I'd hate to find out too late I've become a one-hit wonder." He pressed little kisses to her forehead, cheeks, and the tip of her nose before claiming her mouth once more in a kiss so passionate, fluttering started in the pit of her stomach.

For the first time in her life, she experienced true need, true passion. Nothing had compared to the sensations this man evoked deep within her.

He was real, not a fantasy like Jared. This flesh-and-blood male could bring her to orgasm again and again during one beautiful night of pure passion.

Chapter Six

J ared shuddered in Candy's arms as she stroked his heated flesh. Every brush of her smooth skin against his made him want her more.

He had never needed anything as much as he needed her. He ached to thrust inside her, to experience the warmth of her wet channel gripping him as he rammed into her, repeatedly driving her to mind-numbing orgasms.

Gentle hands kneaded his balls. Lithe fingers gripped his shaft, sliding sensually over it, driving him to a desire bordering on obsession to have this woman—to take her in every way imaginable until neither of them could think or breathe.

The time for tenderness had passed. He covered her lips with his, delved deep into her mouth, teasing her tongue with his and breathing in her sweet, sweet breath.

His heart pounded, cock throbbed, and his head fairly spun with the desire to drive inside her. Slowly, reluctantly, he ended their kiss. Resting his forehead on hers, he said, "I don't know how I will ever go back to my empty life after this."

"I—what do you mean?" She sounded genuinely confused but had no idea what his life held for him. How could she?

He chuckled mirthlessly. "Forget I said that. Consider it an instant of temporary insanity. Blame it on the heat of the moment."

He moved lower, not wanting to allow her too much time to think. He didn't want to give her false hope that this could be any more than it was. He could only wish he made it good enough for her that, years from now, she would feel the same—that both their fantasies had come true.

Lifting one smooth leg, he brought her ankle to his lips. Inch by slow inch, he kissed his way back up her body, his tongue laving the hollow behind her knees and the crease between her thighs and hips.

"You smell exquisite." He dipped his head to her sweet-smelling core. "This is what I have been wishing for ever since Madame Eve contacted me about you."

He lapped slowly at her smooth labia, and her flavor burst over his taste buds. His stomach clenched, and his cock jerked. Parting her lips with his thumbs, he pulled her clit into his mouth, sucking hard. With a gasp, she bucked. He threw her legs over his shoulders and wrapped his arms around her thighs and held her in place as he turned his attention back to sucking her clit.

Candy whimpered and fisted the sheets.

Jared liked arousing her, loved how responsive she could be when he nipped her ear lobe or flicked her clit with the tip of his tongue. He smiled when her head thrashed on the pillow and her low moans of desire filled the room.

He continued to ravish her and it didn't take long before she arched off the bed and screamed. Her thighs clenched, holding his head tight as she came. With one slow lick, he pulled away, slowly crawling back up her limp body. Pressing a kiss against her mouth, he let her taste her arousal on his lips. Candy kissed him back, her passionate response nothing less than he'd come to expect from the sensual woman.

When her breathing returned to normal, she

reached between them, her long fingers wrapping around his hard shaft, sliding up and down. He thrust against her.

"The condoms," he said gruffly, forgetting to disguise his voice. Although Jared could neither spread nor catch human diseases, Candy didn't know that. He still had to protect her however. Grimacing, he leaned toward the nightstand, opened the top drawer and pulled out one foil-lined packet from the entire box Madame Eve had provided for them. She obviously had a lot of confidence in him.

Ripping the package open with his teeth, he sheathed himself. "Are ye ready, darlin'? All I can think about is sinking deep inside you and fucking you until you scream again." he said, again forgetting the accent.

She must have been too far gone to notice, because she raised her hips. "I'm ready."

Jared moved slowly. He only had one chance to get this right and get it right he would. He wanted to relish the sensation of his cock sinking slowly into her tight flesh for the first time. He planned to create a memory, one to last him a lifetime, thanks to his damned career.

His heart slammed against his ribs as he pressed

deeper and deeper, muscles clenching, aching to drive into her with abandon. But he held back, had to take this time to go slowly. As much as he wished she was someone who couldn't possibly exist—this woman had stolen his heart.

Chapter Seven

Candy waited for his full possession. For some reason he moved slowly—too slowly. However, her mystery man was strong. He held onto his control, even when she wrapped her legs around him in an attempt to pull him deeper.

"I want to savor this," he said in a low voice. "We only get *one* first time and I want it to be perfect."

"If that's the case, then we aren't ready yet," she whispered. "It's my turn to explore *your* body." Leaning up, she pressed a kiss to his lips. She'd stopped imagining him as Jared Harwell. She had no idea who this man might be, but he was hers for now.

"As you wish." He pulled away and lay back on the bed.

She ran her palms over his smooth skin. Hard, like warm marble, his body could have been sculpted by a master. Ridged muscles covered his abdomen. Well-defined pectorals jumped beneath her fingertips while she explored his chest and circled his nipples, gently scraping them with her nails while her fingers danced through the coarse hair on his chest.

He groaned. Like he had done to her body, she kissed her way over his chest, dipping into every hollow. She tasted him, breathed in his slight musk, and took her time making her way down toward his stomach.

Gooseflesh covered his arms and legs as she continued her slow examination of his perfect form. Delighted she caused such a reaction, she ventured lower, following the treasure trail straight to his groin and the erection springing up from the juncture of his thighs.

Cupping his sac, she rolled it between her fingers. He panted beneath her. She removed the condom and gave him a tentative lick. "It tastes like oranges, too." She wasted no time taking him into her mouth.

He jerked. "Are you trying to kill me?" The words were muffled, as though he held a hand over his face, giving his voice a strange inflection.

"No. I'm trying to make you come."

"Darlin', in my current state, I think all you'd have to do is touch me to do that." He chuckled, cupping

48

her jaw. "There's time for this later. Why don't you let me finish what I started?"

"No." She pulled away. "I've already said it's my turn. Now, lie back and take it like a man."

"Yes, ma'am."

Crawling between his legs, she licked the base of his cock. "It's difficult when I can't see you. Are you sure you want the lights off?" she asked.

"Yes. Of that, I am most sure."

"Okay." Undaunted, she ran her nails up his thighs then tongued the slit.

"God, woman, you're killing me." His hips jerked again, driving him farther into her mouth.

She smiled, gently scraping his length with her teeth, running her tongue along the protruding veins. Bobbing her head, she took him deeper, concentrating on relaxing her throat around his impressive length.

"That's it. That's quite enough." He bolted upright, grasped her arms, and rolled atop her once again.

Her childish fantasies of an extremely famous A-list actor flew out the proverbial window when he kissed her once more. She only cared that this man continued giving her the pleasure she craved, the intense pleasure she had found with him.

He fumbled in the drawer for a moment, pulled out another condom, and rolled it onto his erection. Positioning between her legs, and, true to his word, he gradually impaled her, moving as though savoring every inch.

Candy arched to entice him farther inside. She couldn't wait another moment to have him ramming into her, giving her yet another orgasm.

He rocked back and forth against her mound. It was so erotic, and so worth the pain and embarrassment of the Brazilian wax she'd gotten on the way to the airport. Nothing had prepared her for the touch of his lips and tongue on the smooth flesh. His cock rubbed every secret place, drawing her closer and closer to another screaming climax.

He bent down and pulled a nipple into his mouth and bit gently, while thrusting faster. He withdrew, only to return with more force, his thick shaft dragging across her G-spot.

Then he rose to his knees. Cupping her buttocks, he lifted her hips, tilting them, massaging her with each delicious stroke.

He gave a strange growl above her as he continued, his pace increasing faster than any she had ever experienced. With another odd growl, he flipped her onto her belly with surprising strength. Candy had never been small, yet he'd lifted her as though she weighed less than nothing.

Mystery Man wasted no time entering her from behind. His hips jackhammered until she nearly lost the ability to think of anything but the building release. The mind-blowing orgasm washed over her. Making yet another noise that sounded less than human, her lover came, his hips jerking while his hands gripped her hips, holding her to him. Panting, he groaned and collapsed next to her. Through the darkness, she made out the shape of his arm over his face.

Hell, she wouldn't be able to walk if they did this more than once or twice. Smiling, she turned onto her side. Pressing against his warm body, she rested her head on his chest.

"Oh my God! What have I done?" Pushing her away, he rolled off the bed, fumbled for his clothes, and stumbled to the bathroom, not once turning on a light.

After sorting through various reasons for his abrupt departure, Candy had no delusions as to why he'd left. He had given in to some strange fantasy and fucked a woman too curvy for his taste. To add insult to injury, he'd ended up with a forty-seven year-old fatty. His words were like arrows, bullets, to her heart. She wouldn't doubt it if he was heaving up his dinner. Maybe she should be glad they hadn't eaten together.

Wrapping her arms around her middle, she drew into a ball and willed herself not to cry—at least not until he left. She couldn't, wouldn't, give him the satisfaction of knowing how much his rejection had hurt her.

Why hadn't she realized she wouldn't be able to keep her heart from ruining this night? She'd suspected she would develop some soft emotions for her date since she had never slept with a man she didn't have at least some feelings for. As impossible as it seemed, she had somehow taken what she felt for Jared Harwell and attached those emotions to Mr. Right.

But men had sex. Most women made love. There was always a difference—at least for her.

God, was she some sort of freak show? She'd gone from being in love with a movie star, to having a soul-deep connection to someone she had never seen.

That's it. You're making an appointment with a shrink as soon as you get home.

After several minutes, the door clicked open, and the scent of shower gel wafted out of the bathroom. Hell, he hadn't wasted a minute getting her scent off him, had he?

Candy's stomach clenched and her eyes burned. Tears streamed, but until he left, she refused to give in to the gut-wrenching sobs that threatened. She pressed her fist to her mouth, stifling the cry of pain that sank all the way to her bones.

So much for spending twenty-four hours together.

It was one thing to fantasize about a one-night stand with someone with good looks who could rival her dream lover. But living the fantasy just couldn't compare. This? This was worse than living a lie for a night. *This* was a nightmare. A nightmare she should have expected.

"I have to go." His voice was a normal volume, but different, familiar. She chalked it up to hearing him speak low all night.

He didn't turn to face her, to look her in the eye. Maybe he didn't want the reminder he'd screwed a fatty. Surely, someone like him would think he deserved a perfect companion.

If he couldn't accept her for who and what she was, then he wasn't good enough for her. Still, understanding that didn't stop the pain of his rejection.

Unable to help herself, she said, "Have a nice life, Mystery Man." Better to dismiss him and tell *him* it was over, than the other way around. Life after Canada would already prove difficult enough.

He didn't answer. In fact, the jerk didn't say another word for so long, she might have thought he'd changed his mind and decided to stay in the room.

He didn't.

Candy could only stare blindly as he walked out, closing the door behind him. Hell, she couldn't even do *this* right. Their date should have been one of pure, unadulterated pleasure. It should have lasted a full twenty-four hours. Glancing at the red dial on the nightstand, she sighed. Two hours, and she'd gotten a few life-altering orgasms from a man who'd obviously found her so disgusting, he'd literally run from the room.

Grabbing the pillow, which should have been his, she buried her head in the downy softness, breathed in his lingering scent, and sobbed.

Chapter Eight

J ared stalked through the lobby. He'd hoped to leave the hotel without incident, but of course he couldn't be *that* lucky. He ignored a fan who'd called his name, and instead of stopping and giving her the autograph she asked for, he hurried through the doors and into the car he'd left waiting in case things didn't go the way he'd wanted.

Understatement of the decade. Things sure as *hell* hadn't gone the way he'd planned. He'd desired pure bliss with someone he found attractive before settling down with a woman he might grow to like, but could never love. While aware he couldn't make lifelong decisions in the blink of an eye, he feared he'd done just that as he'd run from the hotel room, effectively rejecting the one female with whom he instinctively knew he would truly be happy.

In the incredible amount of time he'd been alive he had never met the one who could be his match. After so many years of searching in vain, he'd started acting, and, afterward, decided to marry someone the media and his fans would approve of. If he couldn't have a true mate, he'd settle for a woman who was his match in every other way and simply continue with his acting career. And after a few years, he would have had some sort of "accident," left his wife a rich widow, and started a new life on another continent with a different hair color and a new accent. His kind had done things the same way for years. *Fake it till you make it.* Find happiness where you could until your true mate finally came along.

Leaning back, he rested his head against the seat and closed his eyes. The driver knew where to take him.

"I'm too old for this shit."

"Excuse me?" The driver looked over his shoulder. "I didn't catch that."

"You weren't meant to, Carlisle. I'm sorry for the confusion." Jared covered his lips with the tips of his fingers and stared at the scenery as it sped by.

What the hell was he going to do? He couldn't marry anyone else now. No matter how far-fetched it seemed, he'd just made love to his mate.

He took a deep breath and sighed. It had taken every ounce of willpower he possessed not to mate her right then and there. His inner beast had wanted it, demanded it. Hell, he'd taken her from behind. One small break in the condom, and she would have been his forever. It was precisely what his wolf had wanted. In fact, the damned beast had done its best to break the thin latex when he had taken over and pounded into her.

His wolf wanted his mate.

Isn't that what you want, as well?

Of course Jared wanted his mate, but he couldn't subject Candy to cruel media scrutiny. What would he do if the tabloids scarred her with their nasty comments about her size? She was beautiful, of that he had no doubt. She had turned out to be his long-anticipated other half. How could she be anything other than beautiful to him?

Carlisle pulled up in front of Jamie's hotel and stopped the car. Before the chauffer could put the vehicle in park, Jared opened the door and sprang out. Marching through the doors, he crossed the lobby to the elevator. After unlocking it with his key card, he pressed the button for the penthouse suite.

"What the hell are you doing here?" Jamie asked from the couch when Jared barged in. He held a glass of dark liquid to his forehead. "I don't care why you're here, actually. So, go away. I have a headache." Seeing Jared's glower, he sighed. "Okay.... What went wrong?"

"She's my mate, damn it!" Jared paced back and forth then slammed his fist down on a nearby table, the wood splintering under the stress. "I can't have a mate and be in the public eye. You know what it does to a wolf." His beast wouldn't stand criticism and continual scrutiny of his mate, seeing that as a constant threat to her safety and emotional well-being. Not to mention what it could do to their offspring.

"Aye," Jamie agreed. "I'm aware. And make him dangerously jealous."

"I could also turn into an animal when other men are around. Hell...." Jared speared his fingers through his hair. "My wolf would tear apart the first man who cast aspersions on her."

"Seeing as you're here and not there," Jamie frowned. "I take it you didn't finish the deed."

"Of course I didn't. 1Night Stand supplied condoms." Jared couldn't spread or catch human

STDs, but Candy didn't know that. "I don't think Candy would have continued without them." He ripped off his jacket and snarled. "I showered, and I can still smell her. Her scent will drive me crazy if I don't eventually claim her."

"Then go claim her."

Jamie's suggestion seemed so simple. It should have been as uncomplicated as it seemed.

"You've already given me all of the reasons why I can't." Jared caught a glimpse of himself in a mirror as he turned toward the other man. *I look like a lovesick teenager*. He didn't give a damn. "You said it yourself. The media will tear her apart."

"Maybe *she* should be the one to decide that." Jamie crossed his arms. "She might be stronger than you think. She's obviously strong enough to be your mate."

"Why the sudden change of heart? Yesterday, you were warning me off her."

"You're my best friend. I love you like a brother. But sometimes you're an idiot." Jamie stood and walked across the room. "I didn't want you to enter into a relationship with a woman like her based on mutual attraction alone. It wouldn't have been a good enough reason—a strong enough reason—for her to put up with what the tabloids are going to dish out. But being your mate makes all the difference." He shrugged. "Besides, don't I remember you claiming you would give up this career in a second, if only you could find your mate?" He waved his arm toward the door. "Well, you know where she is. You should go get her before she gets away."

Jared couldn't believe how stupid he'd been. "You're right." But first, he had to take care of his career. It's a damned good thing he hadn't signed the contract for the new movie his agent had been nagging him to do. He'd planned to take the year off and look for the woman he intended to marry and adopt children with. Having children of his own was impossible because the only woman he could impregnate was his mate. And since he'd never thought he'd find her, at least not anytime soon....

He grinned. "Won't she be surprised to find out as soon as she's mine, she'll have our longevity and become as fertile as she was in her twenties?"

"You'd better hope she even wants kids with you. Any female in her right mind might balk at having babies by someone with your ugly mug." Jamie laughed at his own joke.

"Fuck off and die."

"You first." Jamie grew serious then. "Now, what do you plan to do?"

Leave it to him to keep me on task. "I'll need your help, if you don't mind."

"You've got it." He clapped a hand on Jared's shoulder. "Nothing would please me more than seeing you mated. It gives me hope for myself."

"First, I need you to tell the romance conference event planners that my scheduled guest appearance is going to be an exclusive press conference. That way, I'll be fulfilling my appearance obligations and let their conference make history. Make sure you invite the press to show up."

Jamie gave him a bewildered look. "A press conference?"

Jared nodded and rubbed his hands together, finally feeling like he had some control in his life. "Yes. No matter what, my twenty-four hours with Candy aren't up yet, and I want to settle this before time runs out...."

Chapter Nine

The high-pitched shriek carried over the excited crowd. "Jared Harwell is the special guest? He's coming *here?*" A throng of excited women filled the lobby as they waited to catch a glimpse of him.

Candy froze mid-step. *Jared Harwell?*

"This is going to be the best convention I've ever attended," another cried as she stared off into space, holding her hands clasped beneath her chin. "Who could have guessed Jared Harwell would be our special guest. And now he's holding a press conference *here?*" She glanced at one of her companions. "What could he possibly have to announce that's so important?"

Candy couldn't move, couldn't process any more surprises. In the last two days, she'd had a man show up on her doorstep with instructions for meeting her

1Night Stand date, been whisked off to Ottawa and landed in the middle of some romance convention, agreed to meet a man to take the place of her mystery dream man—a stand-in for Jared Harwell, no less—the mystery dream man dumped her after only a couple of hours of earth-shattering sex, and now her *real dream man* was somewhere in the building? Could her life get any more ironic or twisted than this?

"It's probably some sort of publicity stunt for a movie he's just signed on to do," another woman said. "I, for one, will be sitting next to the pool. The man doesn't impress me a bit. He puts his pants on one leg at a time, just like the rest of us." She snorted. "If I ask for his autograph at all, it will be for my sister. She's even named her GPS after him." She turned to walk away then added, "Unless something exciting happens like he announces his retirement, don't bother me."

Candy stared, mouth agape, as the woman strode away without a backward glance. Part of her wanted to attend the press conference. It would most likely be the closest she would ever get to meeting the man, after all. Still another part of her wanted to hole up in her room and cry over her botched one-night stand.

Hell, paying for a date hadn't guaranteed it would work out.

What kind of failure am I?

And, she couldn't get a refund for her date. Like it or not, Candy had gotten exactly what she'd asked for, although it hadn't lasted quite the entire night. Too bad the experience had hurt her more, scarred her more, than she had ever imagined it could.

A sea of reporters and photographers flooded the lobby and Jared Harwell entered amidst a multitude of camera flashes and hurriedly barked questions. He stopped just inside the door, his expression blank, his face white as the sheets on the bed upstairs Candy couldn't bear to sleep in. In fact, she'd moved her things to another room.

The expression in his gray-green eyes had her doing a double take. If she hadn't known better, she would have sworn he stared directly at her. Gritting her teeth, she raised her chin. So what if she had red-rimmed eyes and a nose swollen from crying her heart out over some jerk who wouldn't recognize a good thing if it bit him in the ass? So what if she'd stayed in the hotel feeling sorry for herself the rest of the night? She'd finally gotten herself together and come downstairs looking for a Starbucks or something resembling *normal.*

Tearing her gaze from his ashen face, she headed into the dining room. She had no idea his people had arranged to hold the press conference there until the room filled in behind her and trapped her in a crowd of adoring fans anxious to witness an A-list movie star launch some sort of cheap publicity stunt.

"Ladies and gentlemen, thank you for joining me." Jared stood on a platform in the center of the room. He grabbed a cordless microphone from its stand and faced the crowd. Reporters shouted questions and fans shrieked. How anyone expected him to hear them over the others, Candy couldn't guess.

"As you know, my publicist asked you to meet me here." He glanced out over the crowd. "I would also like to thank the event coordinators of the romance convention for allowing me this opportunity to appear and meet my fans, but also to hold this unscheduled press conference. This is *their* hotel for the weekend, after all." He grinned at a group of ladies who returned his smile from a corner of the room.

"They are true romantics and couldn't resist my plea once I explained my problem." He paced across the platform. Thankfully, he spoke into a microphone, otherwise no one would have heard a word he said with the media goons and fans still shouting.

"First, I'll say this; I am *not* here to answer questions from the media. I am here to make a statement and ask someone a very important question." Shifting a bit to the right, he looked out over the crowd as though searching for someone. "I wanted you all to be the first to know that, as of this moment, I'm retiring from show business."

Every female in the room gave a collective gasp, Candy included.

Someone behind her hissed, "Go get Marcia! She's at the pool."

Jared's retirement could only be a good thing. After last night, Candy would want to see him in new movies, and she should probably do her best to avoid that. She needed to let her unhealthy obsession with the movie star go, and the best way would be to stop going to his movies and fantasizing she was his off-screen love interest.

"I have no desire to act anymore. In fact, I have only one desire and that's to settle down with a leading lady of my own. I have found her. I merely need to convince her that *I* am the hero she's waited the bulk of her adult life to meet."

"Any woman who would turn him down is a moron, if you ask me," someone commented from behind Candy.

She couldn't agree more.

"First, I'll tell you a story. It's a fantasy, really. I dreamed I could be happy living this life of fame and fortune, but it turned out to be more of a nightmare." Leaving the platform, he strode through the parting crowd. Everyone stared at each other, trying to figure out who he could be searching for.

"Don't get me wrong. My career has been very good to me, and I owe everything to my fans. But, while this nightmare played out in my life, I had dreams—of someone who could be everything I needed in my life. Then I found her. She's beautiful, though she probably doesn't think so. She's smart, and she is a perfect match for me."

"What I don't understand is why he thinks he has to end his career for this paragon of womanly virtue," one of the reporters said dryly as he held his camera up.

"Probably because he doesn't want you, and every other reporter in the world, butting your nose into his private life," Candy muttered under her breath.

Whatever Jared's reasons were for retiring, they were his own and, like the rest of the world, she must respect his decision to go where his heart led him—no matter how thoroughly it broke anyone's heart.

Chapter Ten

Jared searched for Candy, hoping to find her before she escaped. She'd looked like a cornered rabbit, ready to run. She obviously had no idea she could be the love he spoke about—that *she* was his dream, and a life without her a nightmare.

At least he would end it on a high note. He would retire at the height of fame, never having experienced the media hype of another, younger actor taking his place in the hearts of his fans. Although he really didn't give a damn about any of it. Acting had bored him from the start. He'd only wanted the fame, fortune, and everything that went with it because he had a huge, gaping hole in his life—a missing mate. That was over, now that he'd finally found her.

"Apparently, I need your help." He sighed. "My dream woman is in this room. I just need you all to stand in one spot and be quiet until I find her. If, like I have been led to believe, most of you are incurable romantics, you'll help me find the love of my life." He paused. "I think I hurt her last night. I didn't mean to. Like most men, finding out I had met *the one*, I panicked and ran out on her."

A small gasp from the other side of the room gave him direction, and he turned. "I don't expect her to forgive me right away." He smiled slightly. "But I *do* expect her to forgive me eventually."

"I know I would," someone called from the crowd.

"I'm sorry I made you cry, love." He slipped into his American accent and reduced his voice to a whisper. "I'll do anything to make it right again. I'll do anything for another chance with you. I realize our meeting has been somewhat like a bad fairy tale, and we only have until midnight tonight. But.... Please give me more time. One more night, give me just one more and I'll show you I can love you for the rest of our lives."

A cheer went up at his words. He didn't want that. He wanted to hear Candy say she would give him another chance. He hoped she would allow him to make things up to her, to prove to her what she meant to him. *She* would always be the most important thing to him. It had always been her. He had just never dared to dream she existed in real life. The crowd parted as he neared her, having figured out who he wanted. She sat at one of the tables, hands over her face, sobbing her heart out.

She lifted her head and stared up at him through tear-filled eyes. "Why are you doing this? Haven't you had enough fun? Do you really have to embarrass me in front of these people?"

He knelt before her. "I do have a reason for wanting to do this here." Reaching out, he tucked a lock of golden hair behind her ear and brushed the tears away with his thumbs. "I wanted to prove I'm serious. I have no intention of backing out of this." He leaned forward and cupped her cheeks. "You have hundreds of witnesses and the press here." He dipped his head to meet her lowered gaze.

"I would gladly die before intentionally hurting you. We don't know each other, that much is true. However, I know my heart." He didn't tell her he would love her forever because his species knew their mates the moment they had sex with them the first time. Such information was something better left for later—after he'd made love to her a dozen or more times—after she'd agreed to be his wife.

"My heart knows you. It tells me you're the one. I didn't hesitate to quit show business because it has never been, and never will be, my first love."

She licked her lips, still trying not to meet his gaze,

obviously fearing to believe him, and he understood why. The last thing she would want was for him to use her as some sort of publicity stunt and humiliate her.

"What would *that* be?" she asked. "What is your first love?" She hadn't asked who, but *what*.

"I don't think I've ever told anyone that I have a weakness, a special love, for someone whom, I thought for a while, only existed in my imagination— a woman with long, golden hair and dark-blue eyes. A woman named Candy." Grasping her chin, he forced her to meet his eyes. "My first love is you. It was always you."

Candy jerked free from his embrace, rested her elbows on the table, and sobbed quietly into her hands. She didn't believe it. But, she had to. Jared had said it in front of so many people. Still, a part of her suspected he'd staged this as some sort of publicity stunt for a new movie, maybe a romantic comedy. Or maybe his newest movie had him falling in love with a curvy woman who had a wonderful personality. He would overlook her imperfections because she was so easy to love.

She snorted. *Right. Like that will* ever *happen.*

Things weren't supposed to go this way. They

weren't supposed to get everything they ever wanted. They were only supposed to get twenty-four hours with each other. Why did he insist on doing this to her?

"Why are you doing this?" she asked between hiccups.

"Because, as impossible as it might sound, I love you, Candy. I have always loved you, and you'll soon understand why. I want to grow old with you." He took her hands in his. "I'm begging now. I want to spend the rest of my life with you. Please, give me one more night to prove how much I need you."

Stifling her tears, she finally met his gaze. "No."

A low roar rose at her answer.

"What a moron!" a shrill voice rang through the multitude of fans. "She said no. Do you believe it? She said *no!*"

Strangers glared at her as though she deserved their disdain. She ignored them.

Jared's face fell, and his shoulders drooped as though he'd just lost his best friend. His reaction surprised her. Sure, he was a great actor, but he didn't appear to be acting this time. And he had seemed so sincere when he'd asked her to give him one more night.

After what he'd done to her the night before, he deserved it, didn't he? She had sobbed for hours over what might have been. Had felt less than human when he'd rejected her and left her alone in that cold, sterile room. How could she forgive him?

Closing her eyes, Candy sighed. She couldn't forgive him on a whim. He would have to work for it. She also couldn't leave him hanging and feared for her safety if she didn't agree to give him what he asked for, right that moment. Every female fan in the room might grow rabid if she didn't give their favorite actor another shot at happiness.

"I won't give you one more night like last night, Jared. Not now." She pulled free and swiped her eyes with the backs of her hands. "But I *will* give you another chance." Hoping she wouldn't regret her decision, she added, "It's going to take a hell of a lot more than another *date* for you to show me how much I mean to you."

He moved closer and stared deep into her eyes, his lips twitching at the corners as he obviously came to realize what she meant. "Just how long do you think it will take?"

"Well…. If you do it right, it might just take the rest of our lives."

About the Author

After her birth in Midland, Michigan, Tianna's family moved to North Fort Myers, Florida, where she met and married her husband.

In 2002, Tianna returned to Michigan after twenty years of being a Navy wife, where she began to write for publication. She is now a multi-published author with books in several different romance genre including mainstream, erotica, paranormal, science fiction, fantasy and romantic suspense.

She currently lives in a small town in Michigan with her husband, two children, German Shepherd Dog, four cats and an occasionally terrorized Netherland Dwarf bunny named Babs.

Tianna loves hearing from her readers, blogs at her website when deadlines permit. She can also be reached at her Twitter, Myspace and Facebook pages.